Little Chick's
Friend Duckling

An I Can Read Book®

Little Chick's Friend Duckling

Mary DeBall Kwitz
Pictures by Bruce Degen

HarperTrophy®
A Division of HarperCollins*Publishers*

Little Chick's Friend Duckling
Text copyright © 1992 by Mary Kwitz
Illustrations copyright © 1992 by Bruce Degen
Printed in the U.S.A. All rights reserved.

Library of Congress Cataloging-in-Publication Data
Kwitz, Mary DeBall
   Little Chick's friend Duckling / by Mary DeBall Kwitz ;
pictures by Bruce Degen.
      p.   cm. — (An I can read book)
   Summary: While wondering if they will remain best friends after Broody
Hen's six eggs hatch, Little Chick and Duckling investigate several big, scary
things on the farm.
   ISBN 0-06-023638-8. — ISBN 0-06-023639-6 (lib. bdg.)
   ISBN 0-06-444179-2 (pbk.)
   [1. Chickens—Fiction.   2. Ducks—Fiction.   3. Friendship—Fiction.
4. Farm life—Fiction.]   I. Degen, Bruce, ill.   II. Title.   III. Series.
PZ7.K976Lh   1992   90-5027
[E]—dc20   CIP
                                                                         AC

"I am cold," said Little Chick.

"Come here," said Broody Hen.

"Crawl under my wing."

7

Little Chick tried,

but Broody Hen's six eggs

were in the way.

"There is no room for me!"

cried Little Chick.

8

"Sit beside me," said Broody Hen.

"There is always room

for my Little Chick."

"It is not the same!"

cried Little Chick,

and she ran out of the henhouse.

"Hello, Duckling," said Little Chick.
"Why are you here
and not swimming in the pond?"
"The pond is covered with ice,"
said Duckling.
"Oh," said Little Chick.
She hopped up and down.
"I am cold," she said.
"Me, too," said Duckling.
They ran to the henhouse
to get warm.

"Peep! Peep! Peep!"

"Broody Hen," said Little Chick,

"what is that scary noise?"

"Oh, Little Chick," said Broody Hen.

"That is not a scary noise.

That noise is my chicks

peeping inside their eggs.

Soon you will have

six baby chicks to play with."

"Little Chick,

will you still play with me

when the baby chicks hatch?"

asked Duckling.

"Yes," said Little Chick.

"You are my friend."

14

"Good," said Duckling.

"Then I will tell you a secret."

"What is it?" asked Little Chick.

"A big, scary thing

lives in the barn," said Duckling.

"Come, I will show you."

Little Chick and Duckling

ran to the barn and looked in.

A big, scary thing

stood in the stall.

It stamped its hooves

and swished its tail.

It put its head

over the stall door.

"Oh, Duckling," said Little Chick.

"That is not a scary thing.

That is a horse."

"Hello, you two," said the horse.

"What are you doing in the barn?"

18

"I am waiting

for Broody Hen's eggs to hatch,"

said Little Chick.

"Me, too," said Duckling.

"Then I will have

six more baby chicks to play with."

"Who will play with *me*
when the baby chicks hatch?"
asked Little Chick.

"I will play with you,"
said Duckling.

"You are my friend."

"Good," said Little Chick.

"Then I will show you
a big, scary thing
that lives under
the farmer's porch."

Little Chick and Duckling

ran and looked under the porch.

A big, scary thing crawled out.

"Woof!" it said, and wagged its tail.

"Oh, Little Chick," said Duckling.

"That is not a scary thing.

That is a dog."

The sun went behind a cloud.

The wind started blowing.

Little Chick and Duckling

ran back to the barn.

"Back so soon?" asked the horse.

"I am hiding from the wind,"
said Little Chick.

"Me, too," said Duckling.

24

"Winter will soon be here,"

said the horse.

"Where?" asked Little Chick.

The horse looked out the barn door.

"See for yourself," said the horse.

25

Little Chick and Duckling

peeked out the barn door.

It was snowing!

They ran back to the henhouse.

"Broody Hen! Broody Hen!"

cried Little Chick.

"Winter is falling out of the sky!"

"Yes, my Little Chick,"

said Broody Hen.

"Winter is here,

and so are my baby chicks."

Six baby chicks peeked out.

"Hello," said Little Chick.

"Hello," said Duckling.

The baby chicks popped back

under Broody Hen's wings.

"Oh, Duckling!" cried Little Chick.

"They think *we*

are big, scary things."

"They do?" asked Duckling.

"Yes," said Broody Hen,

"but soon the baby chicks

will grow big and brave,

just like you and my Little Chick.

Then you can all play together."

"Good," said Little Chick,
"but right now I want to play
with my friend."
"Me, too," said Duckling.
And they ran outside to play.